W9-BFO-873

Dear Parents:

Congratulations! Your child is taking the first steps on an exciting journey. The destination? Independent reading!

STEP INTO READING® will help your child get there. The program offers five steps to reading success. Each step includes fun stories and colorful art or photographs. In addition to original fiction and books with favorite characters, there are Step into Reading Non-Fiction Readers, Phonics Readers and Boxed Sets, Sticker Readers, and Comic Readers—a complete literacy program with something to interest every child.

Learning to Read, Step by Step!

Ready to Read   Preschool–Kindergarten
• big type and easy words • rhyme and rhythm • picture clues
For children who know the alphabet and are eager to begin reading.

Reading with Help   Preschool–Grade 1
• basic vocabulary • short sentences • simple stories
For children who recognize familiar words and sound out new words with help.

Reading on Your Own   Grades 1–3
• engaging characters • easy-to-follow plots • popular topics
For children who are ready to read on their own.

Reading Paragraphs   Grades 2–3
• challenging vocabulary • short paragraphs • exciting stories
For newly independent readers who read simple sentences with confidence.

Ready for Chapters   Grades 2–4
• chapters • longer paragraphs • full-color art
For children who want to take the plunge into chapter books but still like colorful pictures.

STEP INTO READING® is designed to give every child a successful reading experience. The grade levels are only guides; children will progress through the steps at their own speed, developing confidence in their reading.

Remember, a lifetime love of reading starts with a single step!

Visit us on the Web!
StepIntoReading.com
rhcbooks.com

Educators and librarians, for a variety of teaching tools, visit us at RHTeachersLibrarians.com

ISBN 978-0-7364-4239-8 (trade) — ISBN 978-0-7364-9007-8 (lib. bdg.)
ISBN 978-0-7364-4240-4 (ebook)

Printed in the United States of America   10 9 8 7 6 5 4 3 2 1

Mirabel's Discovery

by Vicky Weber

illustrated by the Disney Storybook Art Team

Random House 🏠 New York

My name is Mirabel Madrigal!
I live with my family
in a magical place
called the Encanto.

Many years ago,
Abuela Alma and Abuelo Pedro
led our family from danger.
But Abuelo Pedro was lost.
Then a miracle happened.
A magical place grew
from Abuela's candle.
It was the Encanto.

Abuela Alma is
the head of our family.
She says we must earn
the miracle of the Encanto.
It gives us magical gifts.

My tío Bruno left the Encanto
because his gift upset people.
He can see into the future.

Everyone in my family
has a magical gift
except me.
No one knows why
I didn't get one.

It is my cousin Antonio's
fifth-birthday party tonight.
He will get his
magical gift then.

Antonio is nervous.

He asks me to walk him

to his gift door.

Doing so brings back

unhappy memories.

I was excited to get my gift.

But my bedroom door

did not glow with magic.

It was a sad day

for the family.

Antonio's gift is that
he can talk to animals!
His new animal friends
show him around
his magical bedroom.

It's a beautiful rainforest!
The whole family enters the room,
and the party continues.
They are happy that Antonio
has a gift.

Something is wrong.

I go into the courtyard.

There are cracks all

through the house!

I run to warn everyone.

But the cracks disappear!

The family thinks I made them up

because I feel left out.

My mother thinks I'm upset
because I don't have a gift.
She makes me a snack
to comfort me.

She wishes I could see myself
the way she sees me.
She says I'm just as special
as the rest of the family.

I overhear Abuela Alma.
She is speaking to a picture
of my abuelo Pedro.
She sounds worried.

She says the magic
of the Encanto is dying.
The candle has started to melt.
I know I have to help.

My sister Luisa tells me
our tío Bruno had a vision,
but he didn't finish it.
He was scared of what he saw.

I find the pieces of his vision.
It is a picture of the house
with cracks and breaks.
I am in the center.

I find Bruno hiding in the house.

I help him finish his vision.

It says I need to embrace

my older sister, Isabela.

Isabela is perfect.
She can make flowers
everywhere she goes.
But Isabela and I
do not get along.

I go to Isabela's door.

I try to talk to her.

But she tells me that

I don't understand.

She is tired of being perfect.

There is more to her.

She can make prickly plants,

not just beautiful flowers.

I tell her that is amazing!

But the cracks reappear.
Abuela blames me
for the magic fading.
She says I've upset the family.

I tell her this is her fault.

The house shakes and cracks.

It's losing its magic.

The candle goes out.

My family loses their gifts.

Abuela finds me by the river.

She tells me that this is where

the miracle happened.

Abuelo Pedro's love and sacrifice

made the Encanto.

It was her broken heart

that destroyed Casita, not me.

She tells me I remind her

that even when things seem dark,

there is always hope.

Abuela and I return home.
I tell my family
how special they are.
We work together
to rebuild the Encanto.
The magic is restored!

Every day, I choose to
see the best in my family
and in myself.
I am proud to be
in the family Madrigal!

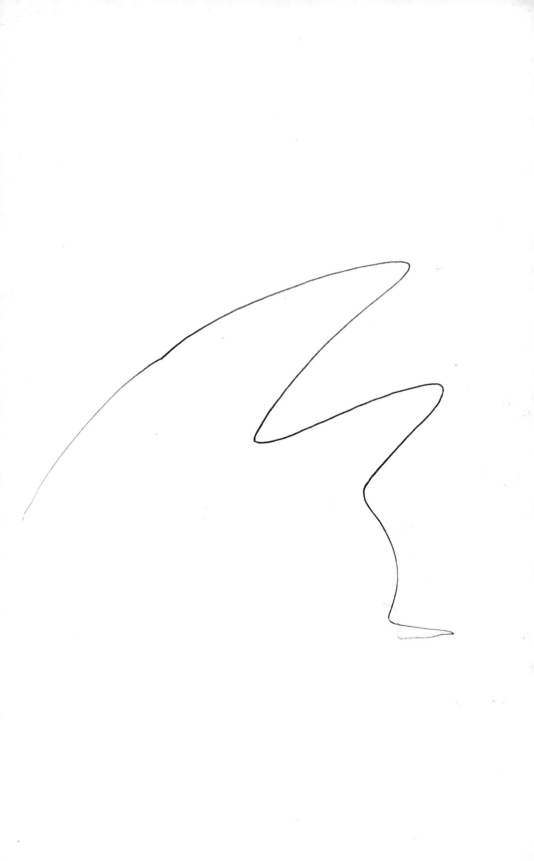